Her Donut Shifters

Mia Harlan

Chapter 1

Jetta

I wake up to the smell of baking donuts. Disgusting, carb-laden, gluten-infested donuts. I can practically feel the empty calories seeping into my pores. There's a good chance I might throw up.

What kind of sadists bake at eight o'clock every night? Oh, right. The three men who opened the Squishy Shifters Donut Emporium right down the street from my home.

I used to wake up with the setting sun. I'd meditate and go for a moonlit jog. I'd play with the neighbor's Golden Retriever. I'd enjoy a bowl of sugar-free oatmeal on the front porch. I'd even work from the comfort of my own home.

Now, I drive to the office as soon as I wake up. I work overtime to avoid the smell. And I send letter after letter to the bakery owners, begging them to let the local coven cast a spell to mask the scent.

But today is so much worse. My boss at the Department of Supernatural Affairs finally ordered me to use up my vacation days. Which means I'm stuck at home, sniffing donuts for two entire weeks.

Unless I can find somewhere else to spend my nights.

Chapter 2

York

I lace up my sneakers and head out for an evening jog. Brooks and Andres have the baking handled, and our Donut Emporium doesn't open for another hour.

With the Department of Supernatural Affairs just a short drive away, we cater primarily to nocturnals. Staff drop in to pick up donuts before work. Supes pass through our doors at all hours of the night. Vampires, cat shifters, insomniacs. They all crave squishy dough and sugary goodness after sunset. That's where my friends and I come in.

I inhale the crisp night air as I run. Our sweet donut aroma wafts all around town. The neighborhood smells delicious, all thanks to us and our bakery.

Chapter 3

Jetta

I last all of ten minutes before the stink of donuts has me running to my car. I drive north and decide to visit Moonlit Falls, a cute paranormal town about an hour away. I find a place to park and stroll along the falls. The air is clear, crisp, and blissfully donut-free.

Maybe I should sell my bungalow and move out here. Or spend my vacation days at a motel I can't really afford.

I consider it as I head toward a brightly lit cafe. There's a crowd gathered at the coffee bar inside and a Shetland pony running circles out front.

The pony cuts me off just as I'm about to reach the door. She shifts into a woman who has wide, slightly panicked eyes. Her bright red hair clashes with her burgundy sweater, and her smile seems a little forced.

"We're not open yet," she says.

I stop in my tracks, and my shoulders slump.

I'm not good with people. I'm especially not good with confrontations. I'm not about to tell the pony shifter that the cafe looks open. Just like I'm not going to storm up to a certain bakery and give those donut shifters a piece of my mind.

Chapter 4

Brooks

I pull on my apron as soon as York leaves for his nightly run. Then, I start baking.

My biceps bulge as I knead the dough. I love how soft and squishy it feels beneath the heels of my palms. How it gives as I fold it over itself. How it transforms as I work.

When I was little, I'd do my homework at the kitchen table. Sometimes, Mom would let me help mix the ingredients. Other times, I'd get to knead the dough. As I got older, she had me take the trays out of the oven. I'd helped her package our delicious treats, and it was the best part of my day.

Bread. Cookies. Muffins. Donuts. I never cared what we baked as long as I got to spend my days in the kitchen, working with the dough.

As I bake, I forget the rest of the world exists. I get lost in the sweet memories and feel completely at peace. It's like meditation, except I create hundreds of delicious donuts that others get to enjoy.

I'm so lucky that I do what I love and make people happy every day. Andres, York, and I have spent years saving up, and now, we finally have the Squishy Shifters Donut Emporium. It's what we've always dreamed of.

Chapter 5

Jetta

"The squishy shifters ruined my life," I mutter as I start to turn away from the cafe.

"Wait, what?" the pony shifter calls after me. A second ago, she was trying to get rid of me. Now, she almost sounds like she cares. "Who are the squishy shifters? And what did they do?"

"They own the Squishy Shifters Donut Emporium." My stomach heaves at the thought. "I hate bakeries. And bakers. And donuts. I really, really hate donuts."

"I like donuts. Especially apple fritters."

"Donuts have gluten. And sugar and refined flour." I tick off their shortcomings on my fingers. "Not to mention added fats, carbs and empty calories."

"You could say the exact same thing about pizza."

"Right?"

"Wait, you hate pizza, too?"

I nod. "But not as much as bakeries. Not that I would want my house to smell like pizza, either."

"I wouldn't mind mine smelling like pizza. It's better than potpourri." She wrinkles her nose. "My ex always smelled like potpourri."

We lapse into a silence of mutual understanding. Men stink. Some reek of potpourri, and other reek of donuts. Their only redeeming quality is that they're hot, but I doubt the squishy shifters have that going for them.

Chapter 6

Andres

People often have the wrong idea about bakers. They think men like us sit around and eat donuts for breakfast, lunch and dinner. I guess York and Brooks often do, but there's a good reason for that.

People expect the three of us to be round and squishy like our donuts, but we're not. At least not in human form.

We're large men, all three of us towering over six feet. We put our bodies through hard, grueling workouts every day; we just don't do it at the gym. We work out right here while we bake. And we're made of muscle.

Brooks sculpts his arms and shoulders as he kneads the dough while I unpack the deliveries. I heft the bags of flour over my shoulder and carry them into the back room. I stack them. I bring in the sugar. I put away boxes of ingredients. By the time I'm done, every muscle in my body aches. I'm covered in sweat, but I'm grinning from ear to ear.

Some men lift, other men bake. And whenever my friends and I stop by the local gym, we put everyone else to shame. We get a lot of attention from women too, but we still haven't found the one. We're each waiting for our fated mate.

Chapter 7

Jetta

The pony shifter ushers me toward Jewels Cafe. "We don't open for a few more days, but I could make you a coffee on the house. I'm Nephrite, by the way."

"Jet," I reply. "Jetta to my friends." Not that I've made any friends since I moved out here. I've been too focused on my job. "And I actually don't drink coffee."

"Don't worry, neither do I." Nephrite shrugs. "And I know what you're thinking. A cafe owner who doesn't drink coffee... it's kind of weird, but the stuff makes me hyper. I mean, more hyper. I'm already hyper. That's why I was running circles outside. Helps me calm down. But I don't need to drink coffee to love coffee. Or cafes. Opening this place is like a dream come true."

I start to congratulate her, but she chooses that moment to open the cafe door. Loud cheering erupts from inside, and it completely drowns out my words.

The group gathered at the bar doesn't even glance my way. They're busy watching mugs in cute little outfits hop across the coffee bar like it's a runway in a fashion show.

The whole thing is weird. It would be a lot weirder if I weren't a witch. But I still gape at the mug wearing a bikini as she struts her stuff.

"What's going on here?" I ask Nephrite with a nod toward the coffee bar.

"You mean the mug?"

I nod.

"It's a fashion show to help Jenny's spirit move on to the afterlife. She's the one in the bikini." Nephrite smiles like her explanation makes perfect sense, and heads behind the counter, presumably to make the drink.

"I should be the one in a bikini," another female voice calls out from behind the counter, but there's no one there. "I could totally win that fashion show if I wasn't strapped to the wall. I won the beauty pageant in Cocovia, you know. My family vacations there every year. Prince Erik himself awarded me a tiara and—"

Her voice cuts off as Nephrite twists a dial on the espresso machine, and steam sprouts from it with a hiss.

"Is your espresso machine talking?" I ask.

"For the last time, I am not an espresso machine!" the espresso machine snaps. "My name is Diva."

"Her spirit is trapped inside it," Nephrite explains. "It's been a crazy night out here. First, the chairs tried to run away. Then, the table started crying. And the mugs needed dresses. Now, the espresso machine has... opinions."

"You're blaming this on me?" Diva cries in outrage.

"The health department inspector will be here tomorrow," Nephrite says, completely ignoring her. "We're nowhere near ready, and I think the spoons are laughing at me."

A few giggles echo from behind the counter, and Nephrite groans.

"Anyway, here's your drink." She hands me a paper cup.

I'm so stunned that I automatically raise it to my lips and take a sip. Then, I realize I've made a huge mistake.

"What's in this?" I demand, fighting the urge to dry heave.

"Pumpkin spice latte," Nephrite tells me. "Don't worry, it's decaf."

"I'm not worried," I tell her. Because caffeine is the least of my concerns. Ironically, so is the sugar and the whipped cream. Yes, they're both gross, but I'm more concerned about the magic.

"Is this spelled?" I gesture at the cup.

I'm not sure why I'm asking, since I already know the answer is yes. I wouldn't have the job that I do if I wasn't very attuned to magic. If I hadn't been gaping at the fashion show, I'd have realized something was off with the drink a lot sooner.

"A bunch of our other drinks *are* spelled," Nephrite says. "Our Mood Teas change color based on your emotions. Our Morning After Mint Delight cures hangovers. Our Feel-Good Macchiatos summon favorite childhood memories. And drinking our Rainbow Cappuccino changes your hair color."

"What does the pumpkin spice latte do?" I press.

"Nothing," she says. "It's just a latte."

Except I know that isn't true. I can feel its magic coursing through me, urging me to head to my car.

Whatever this spell is, it's pulling me toward home. Where the squishy shifters and their stinky bakery are ruining the neighborhood, one donut at a time.

Chapter 8

York

I hand a box of donuts to another happy customer and feel a wave of satisfaction. I have a certain talent when it comes to donuts, and I don't just mean eating them. Sure, I snack on a couple dozen throughout the day, but it's hard not to when they taste so good.

I've had a thing for donuts since I was a kid. I'd detour by the bakery every day on the way to and from school. Sometimes, I'd stop by on weekends and at lunch.

My happiest memories are of standing outside that shop, inhaling the delicious aroma and drooling over the display. I'd always spend my allowance on donuts: jelly, chocolate, glazed, Boston creme. I love them all.

That's why no one was surprised when I shifted into a donut. It happened in homeroom while I was doing some last-minute homework. One second I was me, and the next I was a donut.

Brooks pumped his fist in the air and shouted, "I knew it." The rest of the class cheered.

Chapter 9

Jetta

The urge to slam on the gas intensifies on the drive home. I don't know why I'm speeding. I have no clue what was in that drink. I just know it's something big.

Magic has a different effect on me than it does on others. It's why the Department of Supernatural Affairs recruited me. Some of the most powerful spells start out so small most people wouldn't even notice them. I'm the exception.

I react to spells that have the potential to be huge. Instead of subtly guiding me to their inevitable outcome, they push and pull me there at hyperspeed. The department has me flag them for monitoring, in case they'll one day need to intervene.

Whatever magic was in that drink has that effect. It pulls me toward three certain squishy shifters, and I can't resist its call. I could alert my boss, but something tells me I should wait.

This spell doesn't feel malicious. It's meant to help me; I just don't know how.

Maybe it's a truth spell that will force me to give those bakers a piece of my mind. Or a karma spell that will make their bakery stink for a week. As long as this spell teaches them a lesson and stops my bungalow from reeking of donuts, I'll take it.

Chapter 10

Brooks

I'm disappointed when I finish baking. Not because the donuts turned out bad—nothing I bake ever turns out bad—but because there's nothing left to bake. Then I remind myself that we get to do it all over again tomorrow, and that cheers me right up.

I make my way out front, where York is busy helping customers. He's the reason our bakery does so well. He can help anyone find their perfect donut: not just their all-time favorite, but the right squishy treat to suit their mood. He looks at someone and he knows exactly what kind of donut they need. And he's never wrong.

He hands me a cinnamon twist, and I demolish it in three bites. Lucky for me, I don't gain weight when I eat anything made of dough. Just like York doesn't gain a pound when he scarfs down donuts left and right. One of the perks of our shifted forms.

Chapter 11

Jetta

I feel sick by the time I pull up behind the Squishy Shifters Donut Emporium. Part of it is nerves because I haven't a clue why the magic brought me here or what it'll make me do. But mostly, I just feel nauseous from the donut smell.

I open the car door and nearly keel over with the need to go inside. If I were any other supe, I doubt I'd even notice the spell... or know to drive here from Moonlit Falls. I'd probably carry the magic with me for days, or even years, until I finally set foot inside the bakery and let it do its thing. Which—considering how much I hate donuts—would be two hours from never.

But my magic wars with my nerves and keeps urging me to go inside. And I know, no matter how much I fight it, there's only one way this day will end. I just hope I don't end up eating donuts. The smell alone is so gross, I nearly throw up.

Chapter 12

Andres

We always close the bakery for an hour after the sunset rush. I made us a healthy meal with lots of greens, and when we finish eating, York heads out front to pick out donuts for dessert.

He hands me a powdered donut hole—a small, bite-sized treat that tastes better than it sounds—and I pop it in my mouth. That's all I have, while my two best friends devour five full-sized donuts. Each.

"I still think it's cannibalism, man," I tell York as he bites into a jelly donut.

He snorts, and powdered sugar shoots out his nose. That causes him to laugh so hard that he shifts. It happens whenever he finds something hilarious, and I'm always up to the challenge.

York's half-finished jelly donut lands neatly on his plate, while a second jelly donut—this one fully formed—glares up at me from his chair. Because donuts can glare. On the inside.

Brooks, the sympathetic shifter, shifts too. A lump of dough tumbles off his chair and onto the floor. Good thing he already finished his cinnamon twist.

I lounge back in my chair with a triumphant grin when the bakery's back door flies open. It crashes into the wall, startling me, and then I shift, too. Karma is a bitch.

Chapter 13

Jetta

The moment I step inside the bakery, I know exactly what sort of spell I drank... and it's bad. Like, really bad.

The bakers don't get their comeuppance. The magic doesn't make me scream obscenities about donuts. And I don't get the urge to eat a disgusting, sugary treat.

Nope, the pumpkin spice latte spell is a fated mate spell... and my mate is my worst nightmare. A donut.

I gape at the powdered dessert on the chair. Puffy. Perfectly round. So temptingly squishy. I have this sudden urge to poke it in its jelly-filled middle. Because apparently, my one true love is the epitome of gluten, sugar, carbs, and empty calories. Yup, definitely a donut.

I'm bemoaning my fate when my gaze starts to travel south. Not to the donut's crotch. A donut doesn't have a crotch. But to the floor, where I spot the sexiest lump of dough I've ever seen. I don't even like dough, but this one's just so full. And thick.

And tantalizing. Which means, I'm oh-so screwed. The dough is my second fated mate.

And just as I think my life couldn't get any worse, I see it. The squishy toy that's shaped like a donut. It's round and blue and has a hole right in the middle. A stress ball of a dessert with a painted smile. My third fated mate.

Chapter 14

Andres

"Why is this happening to me?" the sexy-as-donuts goddess wails.

She's absolutely gorgeous, even if she does seem quite unhinged. Her eyes are a beautiful blue that reminds me of my squishy donut. They're also wide with panic. She threads her fingers through her golden hair, which, I realize, is the same shade as Brooks's dough. She tugs on strands of it with so much force that I'm surprised she doesn't pull out chunks.

I watch her pink sweater rise up and down, cupping her perfect breasts. So large and squishy, like York's donut. No, not *that* donut.

I want to touch her everywhere. Run my fingers through her hair. Find out how her skin feels. Not that squishy donuts have fingers, but a guy can dream.

Her gaze snaps from me, to Donut York, to Lump of Dough Brooks. I want her even more.

"I hate donuts!" she cries, and my heart sinks.

Chapter 15

Brooks

Disappointment courses through me as I gaze up at the gorgeous blonde. Maybe she has a thing against us Bayans—supes from Shifter Bay. We shift into inanimate objects. Objects that were meaningful to us in our teens. Like donuts. Or dough.

Personally, I think that it's the best thing since sliced bread, but there are people out there who just don't get it. Don't get us. There are people who think that we're a joke.

Supes respect wolves, dragons, and bears—even cats, chameleons, and skunks. Like they're somehow better than us, when they're not. Others only love big, in-your-face inanimate object shifters. Andres's cousin, Xavi, shifts into a block of ice, and everyone takes notice. But there are benefits to being small and squishy, like us.

When we shift, York, Andres and I don't destroy everything within reach. Not like a dragon or Ice Block Xavi would. And I'd like to see any other shifter scarf down two dozen donuts a day without gaining weight. I'd like to see anyone enjoy tactile pleasure the way Squishy Donut Andres can.

And maybe, once the gorgeous blonde gets to know us, she'll realize it too.

Chapter 16

Jetta

I'm having a nervous breakdown when the jelly donut, lump of dough, and squishy donut shift. Into men. Hot, muscular men... who are the furthest thing from squishy.

"You're people!" I cry like a weirdo. Could I sound any more stupid?

Obviously, they're shifters. How did I not realize they were shifters? It's not like a person can be mated to a donut. What is wrong with me?

"You thought we were objects?" the squishy donut shifter asks in surprise. I long to thread my fingers through his dark brown hair. I want to feel the rock-hard abs hidden beneath his shirt. Not to mention those tanned biceps. Yum. And his killer quads. Seriously, all that muscle makes me drool.

I'm so relieved I'm attracted to men, not donuts and a lump of dough. Being turned on by one's mates is normal. Being unusually turned on by squishy objects is not.

Squishy Donut nudges his friend, the blond, broad-shouldered hunk who shifted into a lump of dough. When their shoulders touch, I swallow hard. Then I zero in on Lump of Dough's huge biceps. And his giant hands. Not to mention his long fingers. I want them on me. Bad. But hey, at least I'm no longer getting wet from staring at a lump of dough.

"You really didn't know we were shifters?" he asks.

My cheeks heat. Could be embarrassment, could be arousal. I don't really care.

The bottom line is my mates are men. And, better yet, they're hot.

Jelly Donut isn't quite as built as the other two, but he's tall and lean and muscular and oh-so sexy. He's also examining me in a way that makes my stomach lurch. Then again, he is a donut... sort of... and thinking about donuts always makes me ill.

I can't say I'm not disappointed that my mates shift into dough and donuts... but at least, they're men. Good-looking, muscular men. Men I wouldn't mind spending my vacation getting to know. Preferably naked. Somewhere that doesn't reek of donuts.

What are they even doing at the Squishy Shifters Donut Emporium? Wait a minute! "No. Oh God, no!"

"What's wrong?" Squishy Donut grabs my shoulders and helps me into a chair. He starts rubbing my back in slow, soft circles. I think he's trying to calm me down, but all I can think about is how he's here, in the Donut Emporium's back room.

"You guys are the Squishy Shifters." I frown.

Squishy Donut nods. "I'm Andres." He gestures at Jelly Donut. "That's York. And that"—he nudges Lump of Dough—"is Brooks."

"I'm Jet," I tell him. I don't add that my friends call me Jetta. I'm too distracted by three irrefutable facts.

"You own this place. You ruined my life. And I *hate* donuts!"

Chapter 17

Brooks

"How can anyone *hate* donuts?" I demand. Then, it hits me.

My mate's name is Jet. *The* Jet. Jet Bower, the man—at least, we thought Jet was a man—who kept writing us letters about how our donuts stink. The one who wanted us to hire a witch to make our bakery scent-free.

We've had a visit from the city and the local coven because of *her*. Because she accused us of forcing innocent people out of their homes, when the smell is what brings in customers by the dozen.

Baking is my life, and my mate tried to ruin the business of my dreams. How can I ever be with her—how can the three of us ever be with her—when she hates everything about us?

Chapter 18

York

"You don't actually hate donuts, Jet," I tell her gently. "Guys, she doesn't actually hate donuts."

Andres sighs in relief.

Brooks furrows his brows in doubt.

Jet shakes her head. "I go by Jetta. And I definitely hate donuts." She wrinkles her nose in disgust. "They're made of gluten, and sugar, and empty—"

"Jetta," I interrupt, taking her hand in mine, "let me prove to you that you love donuts."

I reach past her, and she swallows hard. Her pupils dilate, proving that she's into me. Proving that this will work.

I pick up a jelly donut, and poor Jetta looks like she might throw up. If I make her eat it, she just might.

"Are you sure about this?" Brooks asks.

I nod. "Jetta, please, trust me. My talent is finding anyone their perfect donut, including you."

Jetta purses her lips and lets out a heavy sigh. "Fine. I'll eat the donut. But if I throw up, it's on you."

"You won't throw up." Then, I take her finger, dip it in the delicious jelly, and suck it slowly into my mouth.

Chapter 19

Jetta

When York's hot mouth closes around my index finger, I feel it straight down to my core. He sucks on it. He swirls his tongue. He licks every bit of jelly off.

I can't help it. I moan.

"You *love* donuts," York says. Then he dips my finger into the donut one more time. He takes his time licking the jelly off. He sucks my finger into his mouth and makes sure there isn't a trace of sticky sugar left. Then he grins. "Just admit it, Jetta. You want me to cover every part of you with donuts. You want Andres to rub a chocolate glaze on your nipples and clean them up with his tongue."

I moan. So does Andres.

"You want Brooks to sprinkle powdered sugar on your clit and—"

I gasp. Brooks groans. And I can't take it anymore.

I yank York toward me so hard he nearly loses his balance. Then, I claim his mouth in a fiery kiss.

When our lips touch, my entire body ignites. Part of it is that York's my mate. Part of it is that he really knows how to kiss. Mostly, it's the thought of these three hot, delicious bakers licking donuts off every part of me.

I always thought I hated donuts. I always thought desserts were just empty calories. Now, I finally understand.

Donuts bring people pleasure. They can bring me pleasure. As long as I'm not the one eating them.

Chapter 20

Brooks

The thought of licking powdered sugar off my mate makes my brain short circuit.

I no longer care that she wrote those letters. So she tried to ruin our business. It didn't work. She was wrong.

I have my bakery. I get to work with dough every day. And the best thing in the world just happened. I learned that baking turns my mate on. I saw it on her face right before she kissed my friend.

I'm not jealous that she kissed York—if anything, I'm relieved. I've always worried the three of us would end up with women who didn't get along. That it would put a wedge between us. Strain our friendship. Ruin everything we've built.

My friends and I share a business. We share a house. We share everything. So it makes sense that we'd share a mate, too. And nothing in this world will ever beat the sight of her getting turned on when York mentioned chocolate glaze and powdered sugar.

I want to bake all my favorite treats, rub them all over Jetta's naked body, and lick her clean. I want to try different recipes just to see how they taste on her nipples and clit. Now *that* would make my life complete.

Chapter 21

Jetta

Andres scoops me up and carries me to the worktable. He peels off my sweater while York heads into the donut shop and grabs a tray of donuts. When I see them—Boston creme, powdered, lemon filled, chocolate, chocolate glaze—I don't feel disgust. I don't even care about the smell. I'm too turned on.

I also know, beyond a shadow of a doubt, that I do like donuts. Because I don't have to eat a single one. My mates will. And I'm going to enjoy every moment.

They surround me—three hot, muscular, shirtless bakers—and my eyes rove over their bodies like they're the most delicious desserts. My type of desserts.

I never thought that bulging muscles could belong to bakers. And I never imagined that the sight of donuts could make me this turned on. I think I'm going to melt.

Andres runs a hand through my hair and sweeps it to the side. Then he picks up a glazed donut and presses it against my neck. It's sticky, and the chocolate melts against my skin. But all I care about is which of my mates will be the one to lick it off.

Chapter 22

York

I've always loved being able to tell exactly which donut each person needs... but I never thought I'd be able to use my talents like this.

Somehow, implicitly, I know which donut should go where on Jetta's body. Just like I know which one of us should be the one to lick it off.

Andres runs his hands all over our mate's body while he licks the chocolate off. When he's done, we remove Jetta's clothes and put our delicious donuts to good use.

I take the lemon donut, break it in half, and spread the yellow filling over Jetta's nipples. I gesture for Andres to lick it off one, and hand the donut to a grinning Brooks. He pops it in his mouth while I lean in and pull her right nipple into my mouth.

Jetta moans. And when we're done, she's trembling in our arms.

I grin and grab a cinnamon twist. I hand it to Brooks and gesture between Jetta's legs, but he looks confused.

"You want me to stick that inside her?" he asks.

Jetta's eyes widen in   a mix of horror, curiosity, and desire.

I start to laugh. "No, don't stick it inside her. You... you..." I snort and then I shift.

Chapter 23

Andres

York shifts, so of course Brooks does, too. It leaves just me with Jetta, and I run my hands all over her delectable body, enjoying the ripples of pleasure I feel when I touch her soft, warm skin.

I love the tactile powers that come with shifting into a squishy donut. I can feel Jetta's pleasure everywhere I touch. I want to spend the rest of my life like this, exploring her body, learning what feels good. Because every touch and lick that pleases her also pleases me.

My hand glides down her stomach to her navel, but the pleasure's muted when her attention moves to my friends.

"Why did they shift?" She frowns at them, and then at me.

"York shifts when he laughs, and Brooks is a sympathetic shifter," I explain.

"A what?"

"He shifts whenever someone else around him shifts."

"Oh." She bites her lower lip. "What about you?"

"I only shift when startled. And nothing's going to startle me while I have you naked like this."

Chapter 24

Jetta

I have so many questions for my mates. I want to know why they shift into the forms they do. I'm curious what it feels like to be a donut, dough, or squishy. I wonder what would happen if I tried to lick or bite their shifted forms—not that I ever would. And I want to learn about the guys themselves. Their lives. Their hobbies. Their personalities.

Dozens of questions race through my mind, but Andres distracts me with his expert touch. I moan. There'll be plenty of time to get to know them later. I've got two weeks of vacation left, and my mates and I have the rest of our lives.

Andres swirls his finger around my belly button and shivers. Like the touch gives him pleasure, too. His fingers glide lower, groaning as he teases me, until I don't think I can take anymore.

Then my other two mates finally shift back.

"Lick the textured sugar off the cinnamon twist," York tells Brooks. "Then lick Jetta's clit."

The textured sugar sends wave after wave of pleasure coursing through me. My arousal builds until Brooks and his expert tongue are all I can think about.

York rubs a toasted coconut donut over my nipples. Its rough, textured exterior turns me on so much that I shatter with the biggest, most amazing orgasm of my life.

After that, it's a mix of donuts, orgasms, and three bakers who really are as sexy as the donuts they bake.

Brooks grabs some condoms. Andres lowers me from the worktable and turns us so that my back is to him. He slips on protection and slides inside me from behind while I hold on to the muscular Brooks.

Andres fucks me, over and over. His hands travel up and down my body, focusing on the most sensitive spots as I beg for more.

I'm on the verge of another orgasm when York grabs an apple fritter—a sticky, textured donut—and rubs along my inner thighs. Brooks grins and gets on his knees to lick the sugar off, while York rubs a powdered donut on my nipple and covers it with his tongue.

I come again, and Andres lets out a groan and shatters inside me. Brooks takes his place, and more donuts come into play. So many that I soon lose track. All I know is that each one has a different texture and a different feel, and there are so many places on my body the guys can lick them off of.

York puts on a condom last, and I lose count of orgasms like I lose count of donuts. But in the end, my mates are satisfied, I'm satisfied, and all the donuts have been eaten. Thankfully, not by me.

Epilogue

Jetta

The next evening, I wake up an hour before sunset. My bedroom smells like donuts, but for the first time since the Squishy Shifters Donut Emporium opened its doors, I don't feel like throwing up. Instead, I'm turned on.

I grab the first outfit I can find—and some sexy lingerie—and jump into my car. Then I drive back to Jewels Cafe in Moonlit Falls. My shifters and I aren't meeting up for several hours, and there's no way I can wait for them in town. Not when it smells like donuts. After last night, I don't think I'll ever be able to pass a bakery—or look at a donut—without thinking about sex.

It's a good thing I have three donut shifter mates that can satisfy me, and they have an endless supply of donuts for all of us to enjoy.

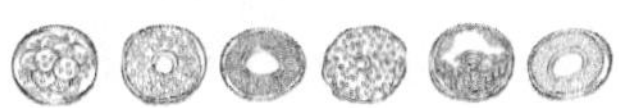

Thank you for reading HER DONUT SHIFTERS. I hope you loved spending time with Jetta and her delicious mates. If you're looking for more scrumptious shifters with plenty of spice, you're going to love **HER PASTRY SHIFTERS**, an accidental roommate, multiple mate romcom with a pastry shifting twist. **One-click to read HER PASTRY SHIFTERS by Mia Harlan today.**

You can also join the Miaverse community to get exclusive access to all the things I haven't published. That deleted scene I wrote after a sleepless night taking care of my sick toddler? You got it. That werewolf novel that's on chapter 59 and still going? The Miaverse community is reading it first. The spicy short where a guy shifts into a grocery store? Don't ask what I was thinking, but if you do to read it, let me know what you think! And aside from all the 'Hot Mess' benefits, you'll also get early access to all my books before they get published, the ability to ask me anything, and opportunities to hang out over zoom. Join the Miaverse community: patreon.com/miaverse

Looking for more unique shifters?

- Amber can shift into anyone she meets and one of her fated mates Chase is a bunny shifter with a rather substantial carrot in AMBER BY MIA HALRAN

- Violet can shift into anyone she meets and is forced to spend an 80-year-old body in VIOLET BY MIA HARLAN.

- Wynter's mate Xavi shifts into a block of

ice and her other mate Leith can shift into anyone he meets in WYNTER BY MIA HARLAN

- Diva's spirit is trapped in an espresso machine, and her fated mates are a raccoon shifter, possum shifter, skunk shifter, and rat shifter in AN ESPRESSO MACHINE'S GUIDE TO LOVE AND MISCHIEF BY MIA HARLAN AND EVA DELANEY

- Neph is a pony shifter, and one of her mates' spirit is trapped in another one of her mates' cocks in MOONLIT NEPHRITE BY MIA HARLAN AND EVA DELANEY

About Mia Harlan

Mia is a USA Today & International Bestselling Author who writes quirky romance guaranteed to make you laugh.

A librarian by day and author by night, she lives in Canada with her husband (who's definitely NOT a vampire) and their Mini Mortal (who doesn't have fangs).

Sign up for Mia's Patreon for exclusive content and early access to future books: **patreon.com/miaverse**

Also By Mia Harlan

Shifter Bay Reading Order

Enter a world like no other, and fall in love at first sight with unique, quirky shifters.

Her Donut Shifters

Her Pastry Shifters

Billionaire Rubber Duckie Shifter (coming soon)

Silver Springs Reading Order

Lose yourself in a quirky, paranormal small town filled with magic and fated mates.

Amber

Amber: Deja Brew

Amber Goes Yeti

Amber's Christmas Surprise

Violet

Deflated (with Eva Delaney)

Wynter

Moonlit Nephrite (with Eva Delaney)

Tall, Dark, and Haunted (with Hanleigh Bradley)

Saturn (with Hanleigh Bradley)

Venus (with Hanleigh Bradley)

Neptune (with Hanleigh Bradley)

Other

An Espresso Machine's Guide to Love and Mischief (with Eva Delaney)

Glow Sticks (with Sapphire Winters)

Paranormal Reverse Harem Romance Reader Challenge: A Coloring Book

Exclusively on Patreon

These stories are updated regularly as I write them. You'll find them on patreon.com/miaverse

Alpha's Luna

Fractured Heart

Wolf Trapped (with Emilia Rose)

www.ingramcontent.com/pod-product-compliance
Lightning Source LLC
Chambersburg PA
CBHW022120050726
47591CB00002B/867